PENGUIN BOOKS

Women of the Red Plain

Julia C. Lin was born in Shanghai, China, and received her B.A. degree from Smith College and her M.A. and Ph.D. degrees from the University of Washington. She is Professor of English at Ohio University. She is the author of *Modern Chinese Poetry: An Introduction* (University of Washington Press, 1972) and *Essays on Contemporary Chinese Poetry* (Ohio University Press, 1985).

Women of the Red Plain

—An Anthology of Contemporary Chinese Women's Poetry

Translated by Julia C. Lin

Penguin Books in association with Panda Books

PENGUIN BOOKS

Published by the Penguin Group
Penguin Books Ltd, 27 Wrights Lane, London W8 5TZ,
England
Penguin Books USA Inc., 375 Hudson Street, New York,
New York 10014, USA
Penguin Books Australia Ltd, Ringwood, Victoria, Australia
Penguin Books Canada Ltd, 10 Alcorn Avenue, Toronto,
Ontario, Canada M4V 3BZ
Penguin Books (NZ) Ltd, 182-190 Wairau Road, Auckland 10,
New Zealand

Penguin Books Ltd, Registered Offices: Harmondsworth,
Middlesex, England

First published in the People's Republic of China by Chinese
Literature Press, Beijing 1992
Published by Penguin Books 1992 in association with Panda
Books

Made and printed in the People's Republic of China

To my women friends, especially Siggy.

Publisher's Note

This is an anthology of 101 poems by 32 contemporary Chinese women. It is written by women of all ages, though most of the authors have emerged recently. In a wide range of subject matter and styles they tell us their innermost feelings, thoughts, fears, and aspirations. The editor of this anthology is Ji Cheng. He first selected 92 poems by 29 women poets and later with the help of Julia C. Lin of the Department of English Language and Literature, Ohio University, eight more poems were added. We are indebted to Julia Lin for her work in translating many of the poems in this anthology and for her involvement in many other aspects of the anthology. We are equally grateful to the other translators: Simon Johnstone, Bonnie S. McDougall, Yu Fanqin and Hu Shiguang, as well as all the other people who have helped to make this anthology possible.

CONTENTS

Preface

In 1979 when the first thought of compiling an anthology of contemporary Chinese women's poetry struck me, I was preparing a paper on the subject to be presented at the International Conference on Women and Literature to be held in Berlin in the summer of the following year. The realization of how little is known about women's poetry in Mainland China and how inaccessible this poetry is in the West made me decide to begin such a task as soon as my then ongoing project, a critical work on contemporary Taiwanese poetry, was completed.

With a grant from the Research Committee of Ohio University I was able to start the project in the summer of 1985 by going to Mainland China to collect the basic material necessary for the anthology. Through the kindness and help of the Chinese Writers' Association and Mr Bi Shuowang, one of its former leading members, I met with a number of women poets including such veterans as Chen Jingrong and Zheng Min as well as with several younger poets such as Shu Ting, Lu Ping, and Li Xiaoyu. All of them were most helpful in providing me with their poems, some not yet published. Upon my return to the United States I started translating. Then in the spring of

1987 I received a letter from my long-time friend Mr Shen Zhen of the Chinese Literature Press in Beijing, asking if I would serve as both the translator and English editor for an anthology of contemporary women's poetry in Mainland China. I accepted the invitation with the understanding that I would be permitted to use some of my translations later in my larger anthology which would include the work of women poets from both the Mainland and Taiwan. Shortly afterward a list of poems by twenty-nine poets selected by the Chinese editors was sent to me. I made minor suggestions including the addition of a few more poems by certain poets already included on the list as well as work by a few poets not selected. Most of my suggestions were graciously accepted by the Chinese editors, and the project was launched.

My aims in translating Chinese poetry into English are simple: to re-create in the second language the essence of the original; to transpose the beauty of Chinese poetry into an equivalent expression in English; and, finally, to create an English version that stands tall beside the original. I do not believe in achieving total fidelity to the original at the expense of artistry.

Though it is not a comprehensive anthology, I think the Chinese editors would agree that we have here a collection of contemporary Chinese women's poetry that represents not only the rich variety and accomplishment of a group of very talented women but some of the finest and most exciting poetry being published in Mainland China today. Though some of the women poets chosen are highly accomplished mature poets, many have emerged in recent years and their art has yet to reach its maturity with their growth.

But be they flawed or accomplished, these voices speak to us of their genuine feelings, thoughts, fears, and aspirations in a variety of forms and tones and with great sincerity. Their voices ring true, and they deserve to be heard.

Many people have helped make this anthology possible. I am indebted to the Research Committee of Ohio University for awarding me a research grant which made possible the trip to China to collect material to start on the project. I am equally grateful to Dr John Hollow, chairman of our English Department at Ohio University, for his support of this project. I wish to thank Dr Norbert Brockmeyer for allowing me to use some of my translations of poems in my article which is included in his publication *Women and Literature in China* (Bochum, 1985). I should also like to thank the editors of the Chinese Literature Press for entrusting me with this task of serving as both the English editor and translator of the anthology and for including the translations of six poems which originally appear in their literary journal, *Chinese Literature*. I am especially grateful to my former student Ms Jody Varon and my son Tan for going over my translations of the poems with many valuable suggestions, many of which I have adopted; and to my good friend Professor Lurene Brown and Ms Carol Kendall for reading the entire manuscript and helping me get it ready for publication. Finally my heartfelt thanks to my friend Shen Zhen for going over my entire manuscript several times, seeing to it that I did not stray too far from the originals and making possible the completion of this anthology.

Julia C. Lin
January, 1988

Bai Hong
(1946 –   )

A native of Yutian County of Hebei
Province, Bai Hong graduated from the
Chinese Department of Fu Tan Univer-
sity, Shanghai, in 1969. She is now the
editor of the People's Fine Arts Press of
Zhejiang. She has published two vol-
umes of poems: *My March the Eighth*
and *A Collection of Five*. Her poems have
been praised for moving the readers with
the spontaneous joy of a child.

A Green World

As a child, I treasured a small
Bit of green glass
(It used to be a beer bottle).

Whenever the burning sun
Was about to melt down the world
I would shield my eyes with this bit of glass.

Oh, what a beautiful world
The sun, a flaming ball of fire
Would turn into a mother's green skein.

Weave,
Weave a silk blouse for the sky
Weave a dense shade for people on their way.

Weave
The wind
Into a cool current of water
Lying lazily on the soft grass
Cover the noisy cicada cries
With a layer
Of soft green gauze.

I smile in delight
This brilliant green summer
Is on more than a fancy
Created by my pure heart.

*Translated by Bonnie S. McDougall**

---

*Unless specified, all the translations in this anthology were
done by Julia C. Lin.

Beneath the Grapevine Trellis

A summer night's grapevine trellis
—A summer evening's party

The grapevines reach out their delicate tendrils
To pluck softly the luminous strings of evening
    clouds
Charming us with strand after strand of
    tremorous notes
The overture to the evening party.

Moonlight slipping through trellised vines
Showers chips of silver on earth
Seizes the faint shadow of moon
To weave a theme of reveries
Beneath the gentle shade of greens
Lovers like twin leaves intertwined
The sentimental romantic tune flowing toward
    night's depths
Is their intimate endless chatter.

Children chasing after fireflies
The sparkling sprightly notes of a humoresque
Old granny telling the legend of the Milky Way
An enduring tune filled with sighs and love.

Tired heads nodding into sweet sleep
A cadenced quartet of resounding snores
Old granny's sunflower fan has dropped to the
    ground
Making a huge round rest note, fitting end of a
    party.

Bing Xin
(1900 –   )

A Native of Fuzhou, Fujian Province, Bing Xin (original name, Xie Wanying), lived in Shanghai, Yantai, and Beijing respectively with her parents. A graduate of the Xiehe Women's College, Bing Xin was very active in the new cultural movement during the May Fourth Movement of 1919 and the early 1920s. She also began her literary career at this time. After her college graduation in 1923 she left China to study for an advanced degree at Wellesley College in the United States. Upon receiving her master's degree Bing Xin returned to China to teach at Yanjing, Qinghua, and other universities. Her numerous publications in verse, fiction, and essays include *Multitudinous Stars*, *To the Young Readers*, *Collected Works of Bing Xin*, *About Women*, *After Return*, *In Praise of Cherry Blossoms*, *Little Orange Lanterns*, *Late Clearing*, and many others. She has also translated the works of writers such as the Indian poet Tagore, and also Kahlil Gibran and Hans Christian Andersen.

Infinite Stars

1

Infinite stars sparkle
  In the deep blues of sky
Does anyone ever hear them talk?
In the depths of silence
  Within this faint light
    They brightly sing one another's praise.

2

O childhood!
You are the reality of dream,
  The dream in reality,
    The faint tear-stained smile in remembrance.

10

A tender green sprout
  Says to the youth,
    'Extend yourself!'

A pale white flower
  Says to the youth,
    'Offer yourself!'

A fruit of deep red
  Says to the youth,
    'Sacrifice yourself!'

16

Oh young man,
  For tomorrow's memories
    Be careful when you draw your painting
      today!

34

What has created the new continent
　Is not the thunderous waves
　But the minuscule sands beneath them.

48

Ah frail grass!
Be more proud,
　Only you have widely adorned the world.

106

Old man says to the child,
　'Might as well cry,
　　Sigh,
The World's too insipid!'

The child says with a smile,
　'Forgive me
　　Sir!
I cannot conceive what I haven't experienced.'

Child says to the old man,
　'Laugh,
　　Jump,
　　　What a fun world!'

Old man says with a sigh,
　'Pardon me
　　Child!
　　　I cannot bear what I'd experienced.'

Spring Water

5

A small river
  Calmly flowing downstream
Passes through endless miles of sands —
  Freely
    Solemnly
Uttering no joyous sound.

A small river
  Meandering downstream
Crosses high mountains and deep ravines —
  Perilous,
    Obstructive,
It too utters no joyous sound.

My friend,
Thank you for answering
  A question that has long perplexed me,
Now in the calm meandering flow
A young man's joy
  Starts to billow.

23

An ordinary pond —
  Reflecting the sunset
Becomes a sea of bright gold!

75

Last night I roamed the lake,
Tonight listening to the rains
  I hear raindrops dripping into my heart's lake
    Creating countless wrinkles!

124

It's sundown —
    The lake ripples are drowsy —
What a long unending aisle to go through!

One Phrase

That day the lake was a vast spread of light haze
That muffled the romping fish in the water as
The east wind silently stroked my shoulders,
'Wait! Don't blurt out the phrase!'

That night beneath the sky swarming with stars,
A pair of young birds hid high atop the tree as
The south wind playfully rubbed against my
    cheek,
'It's done! You've uttered the phrase!'

That night there was a sad moon on the lake
Where autumn fireflies flitted and glowed as
The west wind tenderly touched my lips,
'Why do you still brood over that phrase?'

Today the windswept sands whistle in the sky,
The startled crow mourns its lost mate in the
    winds, and
The north wind solemnly wipes my eyes,
'It's too late to retrieve that phrase now, isn't it?'

Paper Boats
— to mother

Never willing to waste a sheet of paper,
I save and save
Then fold them into small, small boats
    And throw them into the sea from my ship.

Some are blown back into the portholes,
Others are stuck on the stern, soaked by waves,
And I, undiscouraged, keep on folding and
hoping
    That one will finally reach its destination.

O mother, if you ever see a white tiny sail in your
    dream,
Don't be startled by its unexpected presence for
It was folded by your loving daughter to carry
    homeward
    Across the sea and mountains her love and
        sorrow.

Longing

Hide away from longing,
Throw on a fur wrap and
    Walk out of a quiet lamp-bright house.

Bright moon peeps out of a small path,
A bare branch
    Inscribes its longing
        All over the snow-whitened ground.

Chen Jingrong
(1917 –   )

A native of Leshan County, Sichuan Province, Chen started publishing her prose and poems in 1935. When the Sino-Japanese War broke out in 1937, she was very active in the National Literary League of Resisting the Enemies. In 1948 Chen founded the poetry monthly *Chinese New Poetry* with her friends. After the establishment of the People's Republic of China in 1949, Chen was engaged in legal affairs. In 1956 she was transferred to work for the Chinese Writers' Association. Subsequently she served as editor of publications such as *World Literature* and *People's Literature*. She is now retired and devotes her time to writing. Her books of poems include *A Symphonic Collection*, *A Brimming Collection*, *The Aged That Is Time*; her prose works include *Collection of Stars and Rain* and *Selected Works of Chen Jingrong*. Her poems are also anthologized in *Nine-Leaves Collection* and *Collected Works of Nine*.

The Winged Bird

Bearing the sun,
Bearing the ruddy clouds,
Bearing the winds on.

Your wings,
The more nimbly
You glide into dance
The more earth forgets its burden.

You've brought the soul's spring
And before my lonely window
Unfold a newly cleared sky of cool blue.

From aching shoulders
I unload my bitter cargo:
Humiliation, toils
And harsh winters in captivity . . .

Cover them completely
With your joyous singing,
And as I follow your music
Riding high on your light wings
My life changes into a cloud
Soaring free in the sky.

Setting Forth

When evening grasses in secret start to green,
A message quietly spreads across the universe.

What is growing stealthily in the dark?
What fire, what light,

What trembling hands?
Ah, don't ask; no matter
How strange the path, forget what wriggles
Behind you: memory's poisonous snakes,
Gladness and anguish, hopes and dashed
    hopes . . .
Trudge through every crumbling city wall,
Let the dying century sink into deep sleep.

When evening grasses in secret start to green,
A message quietly spreads across the universe.

Time's treachery cannot stop us.
Wasn't there the first glint of lamplight
In that desolate past?
Brute civilization now slays our
Original nature with hypocrisy and conspiracy.
Oh, let us be ourselves; every metamorphosis
Has its beginning and completion.

When the evening grasses in secret start to green,
A message quietly spreads across the universe.

Countless lines may be drawn from one point,
A singular point, one tiny sphere
That leads to many greater spheres.
Ah, let no cunning lies
Deceive us. Let us set forth
On every dawn that has cast off its dark night.

Mountain and Sea

Never tire of looking at it.
There's only the Jingting Mountain.

Li Po*

Soaring
Without wings,
Voyaging
Without a sail,

Outside the little courtyard,
An ancient locust tree
Becomes my Jingting Mountain.
Day and night we gaze at each other.

The sea
Every day, every night
Surges in the heart
Churning up waves.

Morning and dusk
A sea without form,
Shoreless,
Retains the same depth,
The same blueness.

Ah, the same blue sea,
The same mountain
You have your aloofness
I have my deep blue.

---

*An ancient poet in Tang Dynasty (701-762).

Fu Tianlin
(1946 –   )

Born in Zizhong County of Sichuan Province, Fu is one of the promising new women poets appearing on the literary scene in recent years. After her graduation from an electricity school in 1961, she worked in the orchards in the countryside, pursuing a writing career at the same time. Her first book of poems, *Green Musical Notes*, won her a national poetry prize in 1981. Her other volumes of verse are *Between the Children and the World, Isle of Music, Red Strawberry*. Her poems are noted for their clarity, refinement, and poignancy. She is currently working for the Chongqing Publishing House.

I Am an Apple

I am an apple,
A small bright red apple.

My smile swings on a child's face,
My sweetness flows into an old man's heart,
I satisfy the hunger of a sailor on a long voyage,
I quench the thirst of a traveller in the desert,
I restore the health of a patient who has lost faith,
I give the healthy a more delightful life.

I am an apple,
A small bright red apple.

I am the daughter of the sun and earth,
I am the chorus of the flowers and leaves,
I am the moon and stars that can be plucked,
I am the pearls and shells that can be picked up,
I am the hardened sweat, the frozen dew,
I am the fire of hope and passion.

I am an apple,
A small bright red apple.

Sweat

I've praised you with such sincerity
— You glistening sweat!
You're like dewdrops on grass at sunrise
Reflecting sun's radiance
Mirroring hills' jewelled greenness.
I've glorified you with such fervour.

— You glistening sweat!
Like streams crushing through cliffs
You cling yourselves to my forehead,
You slide down my back.

Today, tractors dash across the field
A thousandfold more efficient than the hoe!
I see the workers' faces sweltering
With the same glistening sweat.
You trudge close to all lives that toil,
Sometimes you're exalted, sometimes disdained.
When hard work is combined with wisdom,
You are round glowing pearls;
When hard work is joined by ignorance,
You are only tears, bitingly bitter.

Evening Dewdrops Glimmering

Evening dewdrops spring from earth,
Upward from the foot to the top of trees;
Are they truly dewdrops or
Are they the day's sweat wakening at night?

Clear and gleaming upon wakening,
Quickly transformed into good rains,
For a harvest rich with fruits on branches,
How ardent and dedicated they are!

This moment moonlight has lit the lamp
To show me the true life of the orchard.
Drop by drop the wakened sweat moistens the
    soil
Quickening the growth of leaves, the probing of
    roots.

With care I pick up a drop of evening dew
And watch it sparkle
But it quietly slips through my fingers
Hastening to refresh the green, green orchard . . .

The Sun River

Chasing others in the fields, singing in the ditch
Jumping in green leaves, and gleaming on the
     branches

Ah, litchis have reddened, pineapples grown
     golden, and betel nuts turned emerald.
Ah, love's ripe, life's sweet, and desires consum-
     mately beautiful.

Lovely Island of Hainan,* how can you sparkle so!
A sun in the sky, a sun in the river.

To My Child

From the rubbish heap
I retrieve your lump of clay that
     I've thrown away.
By the oil lamp
I begin again to mould
That which I have shattered —
Your dreams,

---

*An island in the South China Sea.

Your small cars, your small house,
Your small, small spacecraft.

Perhaps,
They are too distant
From your mother's needs.
When I went downhill with the hoe heavy on my
    shoulder —
How I wished you had cleaned the house,
Lit the stove,
And steamed a pot of rice . . .

Weeping,
You retorted:
'Why must you write poems and sing songs?'

Ah my bright son
I chew over your words.
Are they sweet? Are they sour?

All is deep in sleep,
But your mother's heart is like
Your muddled lump of clay,
Forgive me, my child,
Let me kiss away your sullen tears.
Let me light us this lamp of night . . .

I Am a Man

If a sudden storm rises tonight
Don't be frightened, Mama.
I am the man in the house.

I'm already six years old. I am a man.
I can raise the long whip of my top
And chase
The naughty wind to the dark corner
And punish it to stand still there.

Today is not Sunday and Papa won't be home.
But don't you worry, Mama
I am a man.
I know how to use Papa's saw and axe
To split firewood for your stove.
Uncle says a man is great
And Mama you do have a man.
If you ever receive a wire
Sent from heaven,
That must be from your son, the great man
Who wants to pluck a bright star
To shine for you as you write deep into the night.

The Last Bus

The last bus arrives at midnight

Snowflakes fall on us
As my brother and I stand here waiting
Waiting for someone to return from a hundred li
    away
Today she must do so many things that have
    to be done
Must travel the road that has to be travelled
    every day

My brother's padded cap turns white
My white scarf grows thick
The lady on night shift
Urges us indoors to warm ourselves by the fire
Saying it's twenty minutes before the last bus

No, no
We want to stand at the top of the stone steps
Stand beneath the street lamp
Beneath the street lamp stand two snow-children
We want to be spotted by her
The moment that last bus turns into the station

We'll take her by the hand, one on each side
Pouring out whatever comes to mind
She'll be surprised to see that we've grown up
We've learned to tidy our rooms, wash our
    clothes
And our homework has been signed
I've signed my brother's
And he's signed mine
But there is one thing we will keep secret
(We've put a hot-water bottle in her quilt)

Snowflakes are falling on us
The last bus arrives at midnight

Translated by Hu Shiguang

Gegentuya
(1960 –   )

An Inner Mongolian, Gegentuya worked on the agricultural farms after her graduation from high school. Since her graduation from the Chinese language department of the Northwest Institute for Nationalities in Gansu, she has served as the editor of the newspaper of that school. She has published over two hundred poems since she began writing in 1981.

Desert Is a Big Fellow

Desert
Is a big big fellow
Only
High very high in the air
Can I see him clearly
The rippling muscles,
The bulging bosom,
The sunken belly

He is a fellow
Unable to smile
Either he's throwing his barbaric fits
Or lounging idly in bed
Truly
A stranger to any tenderness
If
I fly too far and too long
I shall feel fearful
Of flying back

But certainly I'll not flee
I'm a small sparrow
Of the desert
I'm a small drifting hair
On the body of this big fellow
I'm what he has let soar in this vastness
A minute soul

Forever in Desert's Embrace

Tartar poplars and I
Are all the desert's offsprings
Children of that big fellow
But the poplars are older than I
Under their custody
I was born

I shall grow old
I too shall die
In autumn
The poplar leaves
Are my models, constantly
I learn from them
Not to grieve
To treat the past
As calmly as the future
Because I am
A little sparrow in the desert

When the poplar leaves and I
Quietly descend from mid-air
We're still in his embrace
I still know
What hour in the morning
What hour at night
In the desert
Even though no one can guess
Within which wave
Upon which dune
I'm at rest in the desert.

Hu Diqing
(1957 –   )

A native of Changde City Hunan Province, Hu worked in a factory after graduation from high school. In 1977 she enrolled at the Changde Teachers' College after successfully passing the entrance examination. After graduation she taught in schools and worked as a newspaper editor. Hu's poems started to appear in print in 1979.

Rainbow

Though we are far apart,
My friend, don't you worry!
Wait till the day ·
When the rainbow appears,
I on this side of the rainbow
And you on the other side
Together let's grab hold of it
Tightly hold on to it
Then together let's flip it over.
Hooray! What a fine seven-colored boat!
We'll paddle with our twin oars
And run with the spring sun.

Jia Jia
(1954 –   )

A native of Chongqing, Sichuan Prov-
ince, Jia Jia worked in Yunnan Prov-
ince after graduating from junior mid-
dle school in Chengdu in 1971. In 1979
she was transferred to the China Feder-
ation of Literary and Art Circles of
Sichuan Province. She started writing
poems in 1980 and has a collection of
poems, *River of Female*.

Women of the Red Plain

Know
That waiting is your fate
Having waited through the season of summer
You begin to wait through the autumn days
The nomads' trail is turning browner day by day
But the men still have not returned.
Those unable to bear the loneliness
Married again
Married men who hate a nomad's life.

Know
That men never feel guilty for what they've done
   to women
Born to roam on the grassland
They come and go as they please
He drinks (often gets into fights)
He dances (often till daybreak)
Married for seven days he leaves
Telling
The bride to give him a son
So she gives him a son
But still stiffening his face
As if she had given him a girl
He won't allow her to step into the house

Doesn't know
The waiting is longer than the grassplain
Doesn't know if she should give birth to another
   nomad son
To cause some other woman
Grief.

Ke Yan
(1929 –   )

Originally from the province of Guangdong, Ke Yan, when young, was actively involved in the students' movement. She worked at the China Children's Art Theatre and Beijing Young People's Arts Theatre. From 1980 to 1986 she was assistant editor-in-chief of the *Poetry Journal*. A distinguished writer and poet, Ke Yan has devoted herself to children's literature. Her major works include a book of verse and plays, *Little Confused Aunt*; three books of poems, *Premier Zhou, Where Are You?*, *Ke Yan's Children's Verse*, and *Chinese-Style Replies*; a collection of reportorial prose works, *The Marvelous Letters* and a long novel, *The World Regained*.

Premier Zhou, Where Are You?

Premier Zhou, our good premier,
Where are you? Ah, where are you?
Do you not know that we are thinking of you?
— Your people are thinking of you.

We shout to the high hills:
Premier Zhou —
And the valley echoes back:
'He has just departed, just departed.
Over miles and miles of revolutionary trek
He marches forward, never takes a break.'

We shout to the vast land:
Premier Zhou —
And the land roars in response:
'He has just departed.
Do you not see over the heavy crops of grain,
His sweaty beads of labor still glisten.'

We shout to the forest:
Premier Zhou —
And the waves of pines rumble:
'He has just departed.
The bonfire is still red over the camp ground,
For the woodsmen are recalling his friendly talk.'

We shout to the great ocean:
Premier Zhou —
And the ocean thunders:
'He has just departed.
Do you not see the capes on the coastguards
Put there by his own hands.'

We search all over the world,
Premier —
On every square of this vast
Land of revolution
Your footprints have made their indelible marks.

Now we return to the heart of our nation,
And before the Tian'anmen we cry out, choked
     with emotion:
Pre - mier - Zhou
The Square answers:
'Ah, softly, softly,
He is receiving foreign dignitaries at Zhongnan-
     hai,*
He's attending a meeting at the Politburo.'

Ah, Premier Zhou, our good premier!
You are right here, right here!
— Here, here
     Here . . .
You are always with us,
— With us together, all together,
     Altogether with us . . .

You always live where the sun rises,
You'll always live in the hearts of your people,
Your people will think of you, generation after
     generation,
Think of you, Ah, they will think of you
They are thinking of you.

---

*A place where Premier Zhou's office is located.

A Seed's Dream

In an icy icy century
I hid in the brown brown earth
Like a small small silent fish
Sunk sunk in the sea's green depths

Fish move freely in the sea
While I rest in my mother's arms
Juices moistening my shell
And a dream gestating deep in my heart

The dream accompanies my deep sighs
As root hairs suck gently for me
And bit by drop I scrape together strength
To breach the pressing layer of earth

I think back to the radiant sunlight
And the broad vistas of the earth
And when I think that they think back to me
Raindrops of mutual longing fall . . .

And I can grow two bright green leaves
To greet the spring wind's down-soft words
I will stretch my loins and limbs lazily
I will burst the snow and ice slowly

Then I will open gorgeous blooms
Each petal fragile, childlike
A bee will circle me tirelessly
And call me the fairest thing on earth

I shall want to believe its vows
Become drunk on his busy promises
I shall surrender love wholeheartedly
So that clear golden honey may be brewed from
    life

And when the wind shakes down my fruit
And blows it to another field
I will melt into my mother's bosom
Trusting that next spring will be yet more
   beautiful

Translated by Simon Johnstone

Isn't It . . .

Isn't it true that mothers everywhere
Love to nag?
Don't do this, don't do that,
Scolding without stop.

Every morning when Mom goes to work
How happy my sister and I are!
Yet when she's late coming home from work
We rush to the curb and wait and wait . . .

Early Snowfall

Last night I dreamed
And dreaming saw a sky of snow flurrying
So swiftly, so heavily
I can't catch even a single flake . . .

Today you've truly come
But I'm afraid to touch you
For you are lovelier
Than any dream.

Li Qi
(956 –   )

Born in the city of Harbin in the province of Heilongjiang, Li became a Chinese instructor in the Athletic College of Harbin upon her graduation from college. She began to write poetry when she was fourteen; her poems started to appear in 1978; and in 1985 her first volume of poems, *Sail, Mast and Oars*, was published.

Ice Sculptures

Warm hearts
In bitter cold of the North
Carved these sculptures
That's why they are so beautiful

Suddenly I realize that
Through love and coaxing of this harsh cold
Even the frail water
Can stand up firm and strong
And in different forms and poses
Manifest the miracle of life.

When spring comes
They will melt
But they will not sigh in their retreat
For they have stood with pride,
Happily they came
Happily now they depart

Oh let the Northland
Make me into a sculpture too —
Into one innocent fawn,
Into a carefree little fish,
Into peacock or swallow
Though one day I would vanish
Let me vanish in the spring.

Old Grandfather

Snowflakes swirl and dance
Suddenly I see again my old grandfather
So clear
yet so blurred . . .

Alive, he was just an ordinary person,
Misshapenly bent
Like a leafbare old tree.
Whenever it snowed, he would go out
And in silence sweep clear a path.
Later, in a way I savor a poem,
He would watch the footfalls,
Their comings and goings along the path . . .

Today he is gone,
Quietly asleep in the dusky depth of earth.
As the snow swirls and swirls, perhaps
His spirit feels anxious
About the sacred task?
So following his footsteps
I step outside
To sweep clear a path.

In the Rain

In the chill of an autumn rain
I shivered uncontrollably
Suddenly, overhead
A piece of house eave seemed to fly past —
Behind me, there's a strange girl
Eyes like new moons,

Her umbrella rose pink.

I'm thankful
But she shyly moves out of my sight
As though her arrival
Is as natural as raining

Silently we stroll along
— That opened umbrella
Is like a wheeling sun —
Toward the world before us
Radiating
Illimitable warmth.

Land

To be a sailor is a man's good fortune,
To be a sailor's wife
Is a woman's good fortune.

Her love has overcome the sea
Her promises have coloured the sea blue,
    then bleached it white
She has mastered
The man who has mastered the seas

Her husband tells her
That she will perpetually rise from the sea
Changing into a pleasing breeze
Changing into shimmering waves
Changing into clouds, into birds
Tailing his ships
To iron smooth the rocky years
All their wrinkles

He also tells her
Every sailor is envious of him
She has brought to these lusty men
Verse lines blue as the roof tiles
She has made them believe

That there's nothing to fear in this world
Not storm, shoals, waves
Only that there be a piece of land in the heart
Only that fragrance will grow on this land.

Li Xiaoyu
(1951 –   )

Li Xiaoyu was born in Fengrun County Hubei Province. She was working in the railway system as a hygienist in 1972, the year she published her first series of poems entitled *Gathering Medicine*. Since 1976 Li has been working for the *Poetry Journal* in Beijing. She has attended The Lu Xun Academy of Literature as well as the Beijing University for advanced studies. Her publications of poetry include the following titles: *Songs of the Goose Plumes*, *Red Crepe Scarf*, and *The Eastern Light*.

Small Rain

Stealthily I come to this world,
Sprinkling so many, many ripples.
Those eddies, wilted leaves, ancient trees,
Those hidden mosses and dim will-o'-the-wisps,
Myriad voices whispering,
Don't disturb, oh, please don't
Disrupt this peaceful life!
And with a smile I sing my song:
Each raindrop is a kernel of seed,
Bringing moisture of air, warmth of soil
To sow freshness, passion, and life.
Tomorrow let's invite the new world to harvest
    here.
A patch of duckweed, few lotuses,
No matter how primitive the organism,
So long as there's life,
There's creation,
There's me.

2

One drop, another drop . . .
All purity, all simplicity,
My heart's a slip of luminous color.
I've come down,
Because I was once a pure and clean cloud.
Hopelessly in love with the earth, green leaves,
    and life.
Oh, a fierce wind brings sand and gravels,
Silt has clogged the stream,
Murky water rushes in,
And chaos overruns heaven and earth

I vanish . . .

When I change into a cloud again,
I stubbornly watch the earth below
Forgetting the thunder, mud, and fire.
I feel only the stir of creation,
Passionate convictions and joyous discoveries.
Oh, look, my heart's still a luminous color
All purity and simplicity,
One drop, another drop . . .

3

I'm coming,
I'm coming.

Some loathe me, saying I'm autumn's cold tears,
Others welcome me, calling the music of spring.

Perhaps I am tears,
Perhaps I am song.

Slowly I'll trickle down pale cheeks,
Softly sing in expectant hearts.

Be it happy or sad,
I'll always be a rivulet flowing to the heart.

In the boundless sea of emotions
I am severance as well as confluence.

4

Gentle yet resolute,
Fragile yet firm,
I've lived and pursued,
I've my place, my legend in this world.
With beauty I've opened every little window,
With love I've stroked every desert.

Perhaps I've been confused, lost my way,
Perhaps I've been a romantic, roaming every-
    where . . .

Some day all grass will share one dream.
Rain has gone, stars are glinting.
Only earth shall leave a long, long memory —
A field of ripening crops, a golden flush of fruits.
Then men will ponder as they gaze into the far
    distance,
Saying: Behold the earth's bountifulness,
How richly it has given itself to us, how richly . .

Night

Under the palms, an island shuts its eyes
In reverie and listlessly shrugs its shoulders
As one green coconut drops into the sea.
Stealthily it splashes up
One spread of greenish moonlight,
Ten spreads of greenish moonlight,
A hundred spreads of greenish moonlight,
On such a night,
How all the hearts go aflutter; fluttering . . .
Dimly, faint thunders graze over sky's rim,
Telling tales about a tropical land,
A green, green homeland . . .

Lingshui County, Hainan Island, September 1979

A Clay Pot
— One of the Banpo Ruins[*]

It is said
That the first clay pot was made by a woman
She carved a
Perfect, rounded, billowing arc
Plain and serenely poised
Upon the mellowed coolness of antiquity

Ah my mother with her long disheveled hair
Enwrapped in animal skin
She pointed to
The purest earth, water and flame
The world was thus born
Born into
A pregnant curve
An unborn babe moving inside its mother
A fruit at the instant of ripening
A sun
A perfect union of heaven and earth
A clay pot

Hereafter all living things
Are endowed with their own fine distinguishing
    fingerprints
Many voices drifting between heaven and earth
Crying out for their mother
And the clay pot
Plain and serenely poised
Upon the mellowed coolness of antiquity
With her flawless ocher
With her purity and honesty
With her overflowing abundance

---

[*]China's ancient neolithic Yangshao Culture was discovered in Banpo Village on the eastern outskirts of Xi'an City, Shaanxi Province.

With her everlasting
Sacrifice windswept and rain-drenched
Drinking in the tender heartbeat of mother
Drinking in lullaby
Drinking the Yellow River overflowing with milk
Drinking in the sound of a bone needle
As fine as a silk thread

When the barefoot mother stood up
To start the sowing of the first seeds
The clay pot fell
Pouring out countless seeds, small and golden
The men

The Silk Dream

Moon thin as water
And watery candlelight
Shine upon China
A sleeping silkworm
Exhaling a long long thread of silk
On a nine-hundred and sixty thousand square
    miles
Mulberry leaf

Its skin cold as ice, luminous as first snow
This great river of silk
With its silent billowing waves
With hidden perfume drifting amid shuddering
    shades of plum blossoms
With its dazzling riot of bright lights
With its soft soft footfall of a princess
In the quiet recess of the tall pillars

With its iridescent scales of dragon and phoenix
   dancing
To the music of bells and drums .
In the bronze mirror
Weave another song of the Yellow River
Another swirl of solitary smoke in a vast desert
Another and another beacon fire on high terraces
Another and another city gate
Volume after volume of poems

Oh China
The China by the pines and beneath the moon
The China of bamboo tablets in raised hands
Oh the China of tinkling porcelain vases
Oh you the silken culture
All that's carved in stones, etched in bronze
The profound soul of Huaxia*
Arises
And soaring upward
This night
In the great silken river
Thin and airy as a cicada's wings
Slippery-soft as waves
Is there a Zheng He** setting sail for a distant
   voyage
To chart out a passage to the far far West into
A rippling soaring ribbon?

---

*Old name for China.
**An ancient Chinese explorer.

Lin Zi
(1935 –   )

Though Lin was born in Kúnming, Yun-
nan, her family originally came from
Taixing County of Jiangsu Province. Af-
ter graduation from the Yunnan Univer-
sity, Lin did editorial work in both
Tianjin and Harbin. Since 1981 she has
devoted most of her time to writing. Her
love poems, inspired by the love sonnets
of Elizabeth Barrett Browning, have won
her instant honor and recognition. She
has published one book of poems called
For Him.

For Him

1

There is a forbidden region in the land of
    literature:
Where love is passionate and death wicked
Where no lofty pen descends.
Ah, death — what a despicable word!
But the joy of love in this world
Belongs to the two of us. Perhaps
It's best I remain silent on the subject,
As befits a proper young lady;
But I don't know what power has wound around
    my heart
Propelling my pen to seek its imprints;
I still yearn to hold your hand ... Because
In this mysterious Eden we are destined
To roam together. Love has taught me to be bold,
    so
I now dedicate these naked lines to you alone.

2

At sundown, on the shaded campus path, I long for
And longing seem to hear your familiar step,
But it is only my fantasy.
A solitary street lamp casts a sheet of dusky yellow
And melancholy, like the rising tide, surges in my
    heart ...
Ah, forever lost is my tranquillity
Since I've delivered this crazy heart of love.
From my eyes you've stolen the key of love
And carried it to the thick, thick forest.
Ah, this wind blown over from the far far away
    places
Has brought me both sweetness and pain.

I fear not its ferocity but worry over its dis-
   appearance.
A young woman's heart is a scale, if one end
Loses its weight, its heart will surely lose its balance.

3

All shy and timid poems
Are unsuitable for you
For you have seized my love
Like a born master, a fierce fire.
From the day we met
You fixed your eyes on me,
Leaving a deep imprint on my heart,
Declaring your eternal claim,
You say: 'The world has prepared you for me.'
And I am unable to utter the one word, 'No.'
Unless I purposely wish to rip apart my heart.
We have no use for all those elaborate vows;
If anyone can doubt our love,
Then there's nothing one can believe, nothing at
   all.

4

Longing is a small meandering river,
And Time's sailboat glides upon its surface;
When love's spring breeze brushes over the heart
It floats up round after round of clear ripples . . .
The water of this river will never dry up
For since ancient days lovers' tears have
   replenished it.
But in my river, the riverbed is already visible
For love's fierce fire has transformed the water
Into clouds and mists of longing . . . floating past
Hill after hill, its harbor my lover's window.
I shall not lightly cast away my tears, because
In our lives, apart from love

We still have work and pleasures that,
Like a sea sponge, absorb our pains of longing.

5

You are the arrow dipped in honey,
My heart its predestined doe;
You are the string of fate,
My songs the harmonious chords it sounds;
You are the multitudinous mountains linked
    together,
And I the echo that never fades away;
You are the forest with no borders,
I am its eternal greenness of life;
You are the deep fathomless cave,
And I the spring water that never dries up.
Ah, you
You are the sky that forever shields me. And
Every wave of light in the lakewater of my life
Is gently caressing your shadows . . .

6

Oftentimes, it is this way;
There's a letter perpetually kept within my heart;
Each time that I begin, it is not the beginning,
Each time that I end, it is not the ending;
It is a letter that never can be completed
When I pour out my unending love.
Though a long separation may come to an end
And we're inseparable day and night,
I shall keep on writing you my 'letter.'
Without the help of this pen, my heart,
Overrun with such deep and burning love
Will surely suffocate me . . . as if
A huge hill of coals needs an air vent;
Otherwise, it will burn to a crisp nothingness.

Lu Ping
(1949—   )

A native of Changshu, Jiangsu Province,
and a graduate of Shanghai Textile En-
gineering Institute, Lu has also studied
in the Engineering Department of the
Huadong Textile Engineering Institute.
Lu has worked as a textile worker as well
as a production manager. At present she
is a reporter and editor for the *Shanghai
Legal News*. Her poems began to appear
in literary magazines in 1970. She has
published one book of poems, *A Small
Station in Dreamland*.

Frozen Into . . .

My pain is a hopeless block of ice
Frozen into transparency only by its despair
And in whose dispassionate clarity
The roaming eyes of yearning and hope find
      peace

If you see it, my friend, don't ever touch it.
What it fears most is the warmth of your hand
And I would not have it melt gently away
Because it has frozen in despair my first
      innocence.

Yes, I Admit

One mailbox, another mailbox
Every mailbox
      Is blinded in one eye.
Yes, I admit —
There's one unposted letter in my pocket:

One thought that undertakes no distant flight,
One wish that reaches no other shore,
And these now play havoc in my pocket.

Last night willfulness and confidence —
On my long checkered thoroughfare
      Open a route of green lights.
My wavering emotions surge forth,
Exposing a bold corner,
Make a rubbing of the soul's true image,
Make the night into a silhouette cutting.

Stars no longer seem so remote
And out from the dawn clouds immersed with
   sincerity
Emerges an envelope, the color of blue sky. . . .

In this moment, I wait between the mailboxes,
Waiting for someone to come out and argue
   with me:
I shall harden my indecision,
And in a second, decisive
   Mail off the letter . . .

Luo Xiaoge
(1952 –   )

A native of Wuhan, Hubei Province, Luo worked on the agricultural farms after her graduation from middle school. She has also been a factory worker. In 1977 after successfully passing the entrance examinations, she enrolled in the Chinese Department of the Hunan Teachers' College. Since 1976 Luo has published numerous poems; her first book of poems is called *The Village Wind*. Her poetry is often filled with a feminine tenderness and a rustic simplicity that leave the readers with a sense of intimacy.

Drizzling Rain

1

Drizzling rain is like a comb
Smoothing my thick, dark hair.
Once ready, I walk out
Into the wild to meet with spring.

In the wild there's a lilac bush.
When its white blossoms brush over my hair
Suddenly the petals in my heart unfold.
Spring blossoms are the language of poems
Written by the drizzling rain to bless the earth.

2

Invisible wind sees its own dance
In the graceful movements of the swaying
    willow;
Silent cloud hears its own music
In the cadence of rain on banana leaves.

They have enriched nature's beauty
And nature has fulfilled them in return

3

Over the muddy mountain path
The drizzling rains hurry along,
Picking up dewdrops scattered among the fallen
    leaves,
Recovering the tender sprouts buried in the
    snow,

The rain infuses its life into the leaves,
The rain entrusts its smile to the flowers,

And to the sun rising from the horizon
It has entrusted a world freshly rinsed.
Upon leaving,
It takes nothing that belongs to itself.

4

Raindrops fall upon my eyelashes.
Like a child's tears at parting
I carefully tap them off
Into the quiet tiny mouths of the spring blossoms.
Child, Mama is leaving
For lovelier blooming.

5

Ah, the drizzling, drizzling rain . . .
You've made the bird songs quiver on new buds,
You've made the trampled grass leap up again,
You've made the blossoms reopen their colorful
    parasols.
But please don't ever let me drown in a shower
    of flowers.

Ah, the drizzling, drizzling rain . . .

Lantern-Carrying Fireflies

Evening fog, like a huge crow's wings flapping
    up and down,
Obscures treetops, chimneys, and water-tower
    tops
Then slowly gathers, erecting walls
That not a hole can be poked through.

But the lantern-carrying fireflies darting here
  and there
Poke tiny holes through the fog to leak out their
  light.
Ah, they must have arranged to embark from
  their little openings
To fly upward towards that vast starry void.

Ma Lihua
(1949 –   )

Ma Lihua was born in the city of Jinan in the province of Shandong. The year she graduated from the Chinese Department of Lin Yi Teachers' College she volunteered to work in Tibet where she is now the editor of the literary magazine *Tibetan Literature*. Since 1976 Ma has published her poems in different literary magazines. She also writes prose and reportorial essays. She has travelled widely in Tibet. In 1985 her first volume of poems, *My Sun*, was published.

Night Song

When twilight's burnt orange silently withdraws
Blurring the rose-tinted mountains afar
The moon descends to the starry sea of darken-
    ing indigo
The night afloat in a glow, cool and cream-white
And we, like stars scattering in all directions at
    daybreak
Chasing after water plants, keeping company
    with the sheep
Ah solitude, only the night can gather us.

Only the night can gather us together
To harmonize the sounds of
The six-stringed lute, the Tatar horn, the chimes,
    the dewdrop
The clouds swinging with the music, long sleeves
    tapping the night air
We gather into a circle, disclosing the world's
    splendor
Inviting the constellations over to join our roun-
    delay
Ah whirl around, whirling from antiquity to
    today.
Ah night

You tender, mysterious, blissful night!

Mei Shaojing
(1948 –   )

Born in Chongqing, Mei worked in the area of Yan'an in the Shaanxi Province upon her graduation from the middle school that is affiliated with the Beijing University. In 1978 she was enrolled in the Chinese Department of the Shaanxi Teachers' College, but because of illness she withdrew from college. She returned to her former job in a radio factory, doing promotion work. In 1975 her long narrative poem *Lan Zhen Zi* was published. In 1981 she was transferred to work for the Federation of Literary and Art Circles in the Yan'an area. Since 1984 Mei has attended the Lu Xun Academy in Beijing as well as the Chinese Department of the Beijing University for advanced studies. Her books of poems include *Sound of Chinese Trumpets, She Is That Mei*. Her poetry is distinguished by its naturalness and simplicity.

Three Leaves

Three snips of tender leaves like three green birds
Proudly stand on the tree trunk.

The trunk sends forth only one green twig,
Where three birds perch.

What lovable little creatures they are!
They're still singing for this felled tree.

Though only three small leaves, they still shout to
    the world,
Reminding people of the tree's full glory of spring
    now ravished.

The Greens

On this poor, bony land
As fire flares in the black night,
The greens also flare up the day.

When will the greens
Forever sheathe this yellow earth?
Ah, in those days when even the sky was yellow,
I've fancied
A fabulous green sun.

What Are Days?

Days are garlic and wild scallions, still sprinkling
    loose dirt,
Days are newly rolled hemp ropes, still
    damp with water

Days are four thousand nights of deepening still-
    ness,
The sound of water rocking in a wooden bucket
    on a mule's back.

Days are the revolving poplar door that squeaks
    on rainy days,
That keeps turning in my tired dreams, now
    bright, now blurred.

Day are a thirst-quenching blue plum, a paper-cut
    silhouette
Of farmers bent with grain under fierce sun on
    hills' plains.

Days are thick leafy shades, umbrella-like,
Skidding down my aching arms to burrow
    underground.

Days are water cans storing up sweet and clear
    thoughts,
Pouring out tears and sweat to choke my throat.

Soft, Soft Her Footsteps

1

Just as I set down the hoe
I heard soft,
Soft footsteps.

'I come to keep you company.'
Through the window hole
Two gentle eyes
Looking and smiling at me.

I was twenty.
She just sixteen.
Why was I smaller than she?

Just as I put down my bowl
I heard soft,
Soft footsteps.

'I bring you a present!'
She said.
Something in her hand,
Moving.

A little blue fish
Made of shining silk.
Ah, what clever hands!

'Done with your work,
Through with your meal,
And still want to read! Goodness me!'
She laughed, teasing me.
Then we tussled and played silly.

'Wish I could go to school too.'
She drew a long, long sigh.
'But my mother has already
Arranged a marriage for me.'

'You aren't going to obey her?'
'But there's no man to work the fields at
   home . . .'
She's as meek as a lamb.

2

While I read my books,
She would thread her cloth shoes
By a small lamp.
'So, get married!
Get yourself a man!'
I screamed at her.
Quiet, quietly she left.

She wanted my snapshots,
One, two, small, large, she wanted all.
Still thought it was too few.

'Don't we see each other every day?
You're not leaving the village.
Are you afraid I'll run away?'

'No one is the same.
Sooner or later you'll leave,
I know.'

One day came a picture-taker
She suggested we two
Have our picture taken.
Ah, those pink sweetpeas
Blooming halfway up the hills.

We had just finished cutting the wheat,
Just hoed over the corns when.
Her wedding day,
Oh, too quickly,
Arrived!

3

After meals
I no longer hear
Her soft, soft footsteps.

'Beaten again!
Her man is such
A cane!'
Whispered my new companion
Very faintly.

After setting down my hoe
I no longer hear
Her soft, soft footsteps.

'She's pregnant!
Still going to the fields?'
There are always new reports.

I remember
How she held the awl,
Staring ahead,
'Shout!
Shout!'
She looked so funny.

Ah, why get married?
Why give birth?
Who knows?
Who knows?

4

Such wails in the village!
This day
I shall never forget.

She was only eighteen.
Because of childbirth
She has died.

So full of life
How could she be dead?
Never to talk.
To laugh again.

On the wall in her house
There still hangs the picture
Of the two of us.
I know behind us
Those pink sweetpeas
Blooming halfway up the hills.

5

Sky has darkened again,
I hear footsteps,
Soft, softly coming.

'I come to keep you company.'
Two gentle, gentle eyes
Smiling through the window.

The Bowl-Shaped Heart

Those old bowls before me
Steaming hot
Float fragrance everywhere.

But all I can see
Is the gleaming sweat
On a hot face.

Under the sun of a young spring
Quietly, quietly
The mountain stream
Lets out its warm breath.

I try to change
My bowl-shaped heart
Mould it
And fire it
In the suffering of our race.

Let such a heart,
The bowl-shaped heart
Be filled to the full
With all the words hotly passionate
That still exist in this world.

Then let it send forth
Its own fragrance
From many many kilns to float
Drift after floating drift.

Yin Niu Si*

Never have I heard such a Meihu tune,** ah,
Such a melancholy melody as *Yin Niu Si*.

Now I know how shaky is my heart,
Time and again it has stumbled on the frozen
    river.

Several times he seemed wanting to cross over
But finally decided to leave me far behind.

At least he still walks ahead of me,
After crossing the river there's Shanxi.

Who has anything to say to each other?
There's only the 'Silver Button String' echoing
    sadly from afar.

Who lets him teach me to wrap rags around worn
    shoes?
Who would let the rags show from his tattered
    jacket?

There's a piece of loose cotton on the tattered
    jacket
He ignores my question, 'Does this come from the
    back?'

He only asks me to step on it,
He only asks me to step on it.

I've never heard such a sad Meihu tune.
Where is it playing now, this *Yin Niu Si*?

---

*One of the names of a Meihu tune.
**A kind of folk tune popular in the central and western
provinces of China such as Shaanxi, Shanxi, Gansu and Ningxia.

Shen Aiping
(1942 –   )

Shen Aiping was born in Wei County,
Hebei Province. When she was twelve
years old, she joined a children's theatr-
ical group to become an actress. Later in
1958 she studied at a drama school in
Hebei; in 1960 she attended the China
Traditional Opera School. She also
worked as a playwright in Hebei. Since
1974 she has been working for a literary
magazine in Zhengzhou, Henan. In the
latter part of the 1970s, Shen developed
a love of poetry and quietly started to
write. Since 1980 her work has appeared
in many magazines. Her volumes of
poems include *Red Lotus, The Children of
the Sun,* and *Love Letters.* Her poems are
distinguished by their rhapsodic praise
of the revolutionaries and the masses in
the age of revolution and construction.

The Story of the Lotus-Picking Boat

Morning breeze with its breath of sweet lotus
drifts
Over the pond encircled by traces of heavy foot-
marks
As the lotus blossoms display their poetic charm,
Their stately leaves, a swath of fresh green.

What a splendid cradle of jade!
Sound of a new-born baby crying comes
Wafting through the years. When was it?
A baby had no right to cry then . . .

I wept
My tears like a gushing stream
Clouded with dense smoke of gunpowder
Now trace the story of a small lotus-picking boat.

It was a late autumn evening, hazy with rain,
As Father went out to meet the guerilla forces,
Mother rowed a small boat for gathering lotus
    root
To wait for a woman guerilla under the old
    willow tree.

Suddenly from the opposite bank came a round
    of gunshots,
The small boat ducked under the lotus leaves;
At this life-and-death moment
Mother went into labor and I came howling into
    the world.

The small boat with its mat of lotus leaves
Was as my delivery room,
And a woman warrior acting the midwife
While the boat rocked in fear.

Mother stuffed my tiny mouth with lotus petals
For cries would bring the attackers
Deliberately she uncovered my tiny black
    beanlike eyes,
And whispered in my ear:

'Quickly look upon your father, my child,
The guerillas are about to launch an attack
Your father has finished tightening his leggings
And has put on his grey uniform . . .'

With a soldier's decisiveness,
My father said to me, gravely and lovingly:
'My dear son,
I bequeath this lotus pond to you!'

Suddenly a bullet tore through his shoulder,
With a quick leap into the pond, he plunged into
    battle,
Leaving behind a small life in the small boat,
Leaving behind a streak of bright red along the
    boat.

Father is gone,
But the small boat still floats in my memories,
Lotus flowers still gleam with hopes, still
Lifting high the torch Father had set ablaze.

Father, a Stranger

1

A silhouette fades away into the distance —
Carefully surveying the lotus lake

He looks so familiar and strange
Bewildered, I chase after him
As if asking in silence:
Are you my father
Why don't you call me daughter

I don't know how you will reply
But I'm sure
You will burst into bitter tears
Because of my convulsions
My hoarse voice
For you can understand
A child may also become hysterical
With longing for its father

Together we are tramping over this land
That has been irrigated with blood
The coursing blue water
Is carrying away my dank associations . . .

2

Mother often used to talk about your going —
Early on that snowy dawn:
Chains pulling your flesh and blood,
The snow enveloping the gasping earth
The villagers in their silence
Prolonging the tragedy
Your eyes wide
You searched for my mother
You saw her —
Standing on a high slope
Holding a thin small child in her arms
You smiled
Blood trickling from the corners of your mouth
But with the chains wound around your arms
    like poisonous snakes

You could not reach me
I stared innocently
Not knowing what had happened
The villagers' tears
Were like icicles suspended from eaves
Snowflakes fell like scarlet maple leaves
The clanking chains
Struck the still fields
In the east, a glimpse of a tall, straight silhouette
The road, a river of blood

3

Let me see your hands
Your hands have rejected yesterday's shadows
Let me feel your legs
They have left that blood-stained history far be-
hind
Only your bronzed neck
Is engraved with scars left by the chains
Is engraved with the wounded truth
I cannot be wrong
You are my father

4

Yesterday
Mother told me again what you looked like:
A swarthy, robust man
With hair like dense bushes
The stature of an unbending tree
Let me lean on your shoulders
Against your warm chest
You turn your face to smile at me
I raise my head to speak while we are walking
Even though you may grow old
You will never be lonely

Our home is just ahead
Look —
The woman with loose wisps of grey hair
Gazing out at us
Is my mother

5

Papa, why are you crying?
Let me wipe away your tears
Why, your forehead is burning
Is it because seeing mother
Has rekindled the flames of memories of youth
Mother is walking towards you —
Holding aloft a bunch of white lotus flowers
She is smiling, smiling at you
And you, standing still
Are like a solid memorial —
A statue that will never topple

Translated by Hu Shiguang

Grandpa and His Canary

My silver-bearded Grandpa
Chuckles like an old locust tree shaking loose
    its blooms.
Early every morning
He hangs his finely woven birdcage on a branch
And closely scrutinizes the little canary,
Still a baby, all golden and downy.
How Grandpa grins with glee.

Up, up
He lifts my stocky body up

For me to feed the bird a few grains
And coax it into sweet song.

Crack goes the branch,
The cage is broken,
The bird is flown,
Shattering Grandpa's perpetual delight.
He raises his cane as if wanting to hit me
But I can't tell him where the bird has gone.

Grandpa, clutching the mended cage,
Sets out with me to scour the woods.
A peep of clear crisp trilling notes
Leads us to our joyous find —
Upon a leafy branch
Perches our golden canary
It twitters:
I'm not going back with you,
I've built myself a fine sturdy nest.

Looking upward at the nest,
Frosty beard quivering and
Dropping little sweatbeads.
Is Grandpa crying or laughing?
Tapping my shoulder he wildly gestures:
Fly, oh fly away . . .

A Complete Lunar Eclipse

*The sun is a heart, the globe is a heart, the
moon is a heart . . . In their mysterious
metamorphoses, they all want to express
themselves fully. But what of men?*

Random Thoughts: Looking at the Moon

Silent affirmation
After silent affirmation
One is lost, keep ruminating
The heart has become
A reminder on a calendar sheet
Fifth day of the fifth moon:
A complete lunar eclipse.
In that instant when you turn your face
Though there's no fond parting gesture
Yet I feel a special sense of fulfilment.

Sitting outside of time I wait for you
Let them observe and measure from the back
I'm counting the stars
With meticulous care,
As if turning a terrestrial sphere.
All the trade-routes are your messengers.

Searing heat is kept covered by the earth's cool
    crust
The silent repository of the deep
Its secret undivulged
Therefore
Let's suspend deep silence
Ah this stony
Darkening looking glass
Sparkling, gleaming,
Is it fire or is it water?
A temporarily shut soul
Is not a wasted soul.

Shu Ting
(1952 –   )

Shu Ting was born in Chuanzhou, Fujian. When she was still in middle school (1969), Shu Ting left home to work in the remote countryside. In 1972 she returned to Gulangyu, Xiamen, in her native province. Shu has worked as a laundress, and a factory worker, but her love is writing poetry. She began writing in 1969 when she was seventeen, and has continued to write and publish her poems in many literary magazines throughout the nation. Her patriotic poem 'Ah, Motherland, My Dear Motherland' (1979) won her instant recognition and acclaim when it was honored with the prestigious National Poetry Award. Her books include *The Double-masted Boat*, *Collected Poems of Shu Ting* and *Gu Chen*, and *The Flowers That Sing*. Shu Ting has described her own work as 'poems that are imbued with both a profound pain and a wakening joy. . . . They are not only the love songs to my country but they are also the praise of love and friendship.' Her poems have often been admired for their subtle and delicate style, their refined diction and profundity. Shu Ting is perhaps one of the most popular and loved poets of her time.

A Boat

A small boat
For no reason comes
To moor on this rocky shore,
Tipping lopsided in the shallows.
Though its sail is split,
Traces of paint are still visible.
There are no trees for shade here,
Even grass refuses to grow.

As the sea swells in full tide,
The waves gasp for breath
And the gulls nervously flap their wings.
Though the edgeless sea
Has its far-reaching domain,
Yet within a small span
It has lost its last strength.

With eternal distance between,
They gaze ruefully at each other.
Love can cross the boundary of life and death.
In the space of centuries
Is woven the enduring vision of rejuvenation.
Is it possible that love, no matter how true
Will still rot with the boat's timber?
Is it possible that the winged soul
Shall forever be held captive on the threshold of
     freedom?

To Mother

Your pale fingers smoothed stray hair from my
     temples
And I, like a child, instinctively
     Clutched the hem of your dress.
Oh Mother
For fear of losing your fading shadow
I dare not open my eyes
Although dawn has cut my dreams to shreds.

I cherish that red scarf, afraid
To subject it to any washing
     Lest it diminish your lingering fragrance.
Oh Mother
The flow of time is coldly indifferent.
For fear that memories too will fade
I dare not open their manifold screen.

For a small thorn in my finger I came crying to
     you.
Now with a thorn crown on my head
     I dare not moan.
Oh Mother
Too often in anguish I gaze at your photo.
Even if my cries could pierce the earth
How could I disturb your calm sleep?

I dare not display my gift of love
Though I've offered numerous songs
     To flowers, the sea, and the dawn.
Oh Mother!
My deep, sweet memories of you
Are not waterfalls, or floods
But an ancient well silent
Beneath the shade of flowers and shrubs.

To the Oak

If I love you —
I'll never be a clinging campsis flower
Resplendent in borrowed glory on your high
      boughs;
If I love you —
I'll never mimic the silly infatuated birds
Repeating the same monotonous song for green
      shade;
Or be like a spring
Offering cool comfort all year long;
Or a lofty peak
Enhancing your stature, your eminence.
Even the sunlight,
Even spring rain,
None of these suffice!
I must be a kapok, the image of
A tree standing together with you;
Our roots closely intertwined beneath the earth,
Our leaves touching in the clouds.
With every whiff of wind
We greet each other
But no one can
Understand our words.
You'll have bronze limbs and iron trunk,
Like knives, swords
And halberds.
I'll have my crimson flowers
Like sighs, heavy and deep,
Like heroic torches,
Together we'll share
The cold tidal waves, storms, and thunderbolts;
Together we'll share
The light mist, the colored rainbows;
We shall always depend on each other.

Only this can be called great love.
Wherein lies the faith, true and deep.
I love not only your stateliness
But also your firm stand, the earth beneath you.

When You Walk Past My Window

When you walk past my window
Bless me,
For the light is still on.

The light is on —
In this dark night
Like a speck of fisherman's lantern.
You may suppose that my little cabin
Is a small boat tossing in the storm
Yet I'm not sinking
For the light is still on.

The light is on
Throwing my shadow on the curtain —
A tottering old man
With a humped back,
Making feeble gestures. But my heart is not old
For the light is still on.

The light is on —
With passion burning
It accepts the greetings from every direction.
The light is on —
With dignity, pride
It glares down all oppressions, open or hidden.
Ah, when did it acquire such distinctive
    character?

Since you began to understand me.

For the light is still on,
Bless me
When you walk past my window.

Gifts

My dreams are dreams of the pond
That lives not only to mirror the sky
But to let the surrounding willows and ferns
Refresh and cleanse me.
Through tree roots I make my way towards the
    leaves' veins
Their dying brings me no sorrow
For I've expressed myself,
I've won life.

My happiness is the sun's happiness
In a brief span of time I'll leave behind enduring
    works
That will strike gold sparks
In children's eyes, and
In a sprouting seedling
I'll sing a jewelled green song.
I am artless yet bountiful
I'm unfathomable.

My pain is the pain of seasonal birds
Only spring understands such passion.
Endure all hardships and failures,
Always fly toward a future of warmth and light.
Ah, the bleeding wings
Will write a line of supple verse

To enter deep within all souls,
Deep into all times.

All my feelings
Are a gift from earth.

Untitled

I slipped down the terrace, watching you leave
By the small leafy path.
Wait! Are you going far, very far?
I dashed down, stopping in front of you.
'Are you scared?'
Silently I caress the button on your jacket.
Yes, I am scared.
But I won't tell you why.

We strolled around the river bend.
The night, though soothing, moved us.
Arm in arm we walked along the bank,
Threading in and out of the cinnamon trees.
'Are you happy?'
Looking up, I find stars swarming towards me.
Yes, I am happy.
But I won't tell you why.

You bent over the desk,
Discovering the awkward lines I wrote.
Blushing deeply I snatched up my poems.
Solemnly, tenderly you blessed me.
'Ah, you are in love.'
I secretly sigh.
Yes, I am in love,
But I won't tell you why.

This Too Is Everything
— In Response To A Young Friend's 'Everything'

Not every tall tree
   is split asunder by storm;
Not every seed
   finds no rich soil to root;
Not every true emotion
   wanders lost in the desert of the human heart;
Not every dream's
   willing to have its wings clipped;

No, not everything is
   what you claimed it to be.

Not all flames
   burn only for themselves,
   unwilling to illuminate the others;
Not all stars
   signal the nights,
   not announcing the dawn;
Not all songs
   Rush past the ears,
   and linger not in the heart.

No, not everything is
   what you claimed it to be.

Not every cry leaves no resonance;
Not every loss is irrevocable;
Not every abyss destroys;
Not every misfortune falls on the weak;
Not every human spirit
   can be trampled and left to rot in the mire:
Not everything ends
   in tears and blood, not smiles.

Everything present holds the future,
Every future rises from its yesterday.
Hope, strive for it,
Remember to place everything on your shoulder.

My Homeland, My Dear Homeland

I am an old, broken-down water-wheel by your
    river bank,
Creaking out my weary songs for hundreds of
    years:
I am the smoke-blackened miner's lamp on your
    forehead,
Lighting your way in the underground tunnel of
    history;
I am the blighted rice sprout, the ill-kept high-
    way;
The barge grounded on the shoals,
Its towline cut more deeply into
    The flesh of your shoulders.
        O my homeland!

I am poverty.
I am sorrow.
I am your pained hope
    Generation after generation
Flowers from the sleeves of flying apsaras,*
    Not touching the earth for eons.
        O my motherland!

I am your newest ideal
Lately freed from the web of myth;

---

*Buddhist angels.

I am your lotus seed germinating beneath the
    snow quilt.
Your tear-stained dimples.
I am the freshly-painted starting line,
The crimson dawn
    That's bursting forth.
        O my homeland!

I am one of your ten-thousand millions,
The sum total of your nine-million-six-hundred-
    thousand square kilometers.
With your bosom covered with wounds
You nourish me,
I who am bewildered, thoughtful, and ready to
    erupt.
Now receive
From my flesh and blood
Your riches, your glory, and your liberty.
    O my homeland,
My dear homeland.

Love Song of the Soil

I love the soil as
I love my quiet father.

This lusty, fiery, throbbing soil,
This sweat-soaked, glistening soil.
Beneath the bare feet and powerful ploughshare,
    It pants faintly
Propelled by the enormous energy
    It rises, it sinks

Shouldering bronze statues, memorials, and
   museums.
But write the final verdict in the faults,
Oh, my
Frozen, muddy soil that's been split open,
Oh, my
Angry, generous, and solemn soil that has
Given me my color and my language, that has
Given me my wisdom and strength.

I love the soil as
I love my gentle, loving mother.

Oh my sun-kissed fertile soil
That overflows with milk,
That gives refuge to the fallen leaves,
That raises crop after new crop.
When abandoned by men,
It never turns against them.
Producing every sound, color, and line
Though scorned as worthless dirt
Oh, my
Dark, bloody, speckled soil,
Oh, my
Fertile, solitary, troubled soil,
That gives me love as well as hatred,
That gives me joy as well as sorrow.

Father has given me a dream without borders,
Mother has given me sensitivity and sincerity,
My verses are
   A rustling forest of longing
Day and night pouring out to the soil
   A love that never changes.

'I Love You'

Who, with tear-brimming eyes and a ready hand,
Inscribed these three words on the sands

Who, still holding to tender hope,
Adorned the words with rainbow-colored shells

Finally, there must have been a girl
Who set down the baby daisies in red kerchief

So that whoever passes by
Is stained with nameless musing.

Sun Yuji
(1954 –   )

Sun was born in the Hailun County of Heilongjiang. In 1977 after successfully passing the entrance examination she was enrolled in the Chinese Department of the Heilongjiang University. Sun has been an elementary school teacher but is currently a journalist with the Harbin *Evening News*. Her lyric poetry won her a prize in the literary competition of the city of Harbin.

The Heart of a Young Girl

I wish I could hear your voice

Tinkling like the desert stream;
If only you would say a word to me,
My barren heart would blossom sweet fragrance.
I wish I might see your eyes
That diminish the stars' radiance;
If only you would cast me a glance,
The clouds in my heart could make way for light.
Ah, I wish your heart were the sea,
Then I'd be a pearly shell forever treasured by
    you . . .

2

When I dip your name in my soul's fountain
And spell it in every verse line,
The whole world becomes an instant miracle,
Rose-colored clouds spring up in the sky,
Stars and moon, as if freshly washed,
Redecorate heaven's blue vault.
And when I inscribe your name in my heart's
    field
Every blade of grass shimmers with youth's glow.
When I, wordless, summons 'him',
All birds fly over to join the joyous singing . . .

3

In silence we sit,
As long as there are eyes for gazing, why desire
    anything else?
No one seeks meaningless talk
Because love that's deep requires no words;
No one wishes to break this precious silence,

Because when the heart's in love, the eyes will
    speak.
Though unspoken, all know the word.
Once uttered, it explodes in air,
It sets lovers' hearts aflutter,
It roars within our hearts . . .

Tang Yaping
(1962 –   )

Tang Yaping was born in Dabashan, Sichuan Province. In 1983 she graduated from the Philosophy Department of Sichuan University. In 1984 she was transferred to the Television Station of Guizhou Province where she works as an editor. She has published a book of poems entitled *The Wild Moon*.

Black Vacillation

Now withered and weak
Now completely submissive
My arrogance has wounded many humble men
My intelligence has wounded many capable
    persons
My eyes have become an abyss
Blood stream contaminated by misfortune
My milk has turned to bitter tears
My drudgery, the drudgery of gold
Seized by everyone
Surrounded by love
Every night is an abyss
You overcome me as night overcomes the firefly
My soul will change into a smoke-cloud
My corpse, all submission, will sink
Into black vacillation.

Wang Erbei
(1926 –   )

A native of Yanting County of Sichuan, Wang has always loved poetry. She started to publish poems and prose poems in the newspapers and literary magazines when she was twenty years old. Since she graduated from the Beijing Journalism School in 1951, Wang has served as both a journalist and an editor for the Sichuan newspaper. She retired from her work in 1986. Her publications include one book of lyric poems, *The Call of Beauty* and a book of prose poems, *A Collection of Strolling Clouds*.

Mirror

A precious mirror is shattered
Please don't grieve, there'll be as many honest
    eyes
As there are shattered pieces.

Tree

One felled tree.
Its remaining life
Desolate and solitary
Is half anguish, half anger.

A tree, forgotten by men,
In spring on its bleeding bosom
Yet struggles to put forth
A new patch of green.

Green boughs; green leaves
Now smile, smiling at the axe's sharp blade . . .

Coral

Whatever the season
You've never dreamed of flowering, bearing fruit.
You are a root for eternity:
Orange-red, color of the sea's blood veins . . .
You lie in the sea's depths,

Knowing only to offer your grandeur,
Oblivious to your own beauty.

Song of a Small Creek

I'm a duckling's cradle,
I'm a young girl's looking glass,
And I'm fond of calves
Drinking my sparkling water.

The wind whispers to me:
'The ocean is beautiful, won't you come play
    with me?'
I reply: I won't, for
I'm fond of calves
Drinking my sparkling water.

Wang Xiaoni
(1955 –   )

A native of Changchun, Jilin Province,
Wang worked in the countryside after
graduation from middle school. After
her graduation from the Jilin University
in the early 1980s Wang worked in the
film studio in Changchun, Jilin. At pres-
ent she is working in Shenzhen, Guang-
dong. Since beginning to write in 1974,
Wang has published works extensively,
especially since 1980.

Impression

I Feel the Sunlight

Along the long, long corridor
I walk forward . . .
   Before me stand the dazzling bright windows,
   By my sides white walls glare and glisten as
   Sunlight and I stand in silence.

Sunlight is strong, Ah, so strong that
   Its warmth freezes my footsteps,
   Its radiance takes my breath away.
   Light of the whole universe congregates here.

Nothing else exists, this I know.
   Only I, secure in sunlight
   Stand still for ten seconds
   Ah, ten seconds can last a quarter of a century!

At last, I dash downstairs, push open the door
And run into the sunlight of spring.

The Wind Whistles

The wind whistles overhead,
Now high, now low
   Somewhat mournful,
   Somewhat ominous.
An old man
   Stumbles past me,
   His hand pressing hard
   On his thick padded cap,
While the wind whistles and whistles . . .

The wind beats against my ears,
Now strong, now soft
   Somewhat sombre,
   Somewhat wild.
A small child
   Rushes past me, laughing happily,
   Sending a handful of colorful paper scraps
   Fluttering in mid-air,
While the wind whistles and whistles . . .

Suddenly I'm speechless with joy,
   My dark hair, floating with the
Wind, follows the wind in songs.

A Pair of Shoes by the Field's Edge

By the field's edge
A pair of cloth shoes neatly stand
To which hardworking man do they belong?
Maybe he wants only to stick closer to earth?
— Sounds of hoes working the fields
Swaths of green, gleaming corn greet the eyes.

All corn stalks are sturdy
And they'll surely bear corn, the like of gold
   nuggets.
That pair of cloth shoes still looks new
With fine, neat stitches.
— Over there who is
Booming out snatches of opera tunes?

As the whistle sounds for a break,
A young man dashes out of the field,
Stout, proper and very handsome.

The sun looks like his giant earring,
— He laughs, he shouts, he jumps around,
'My precious shoes are still over there.'

Tapping away the dust on his shoes,
Then taking a look at his muddy feet,
He tucks the shoes under his arm.
The road is smoldering hot under the sun.
Thump, thump, thump,
Bare feet trudging on earth, the color of antique
    bronze.

Holiday, By the Lake, Random Thought

1

I stand leaning against the bridge railing
The moon swaying in the waves.
Ah, last year,
A night the same as this
Dim and misty.

'How beautiful!'
— Clearly someone was speaking to me,
But the voice was unfamiliar.
I turned around and left,
(Like a deserter).

I stand leaning against the railing,
Throw down a few pebbles,
Wrinkling the face of the moon.

2

It was here
That I used to jump around,
Letting down the little bottle
Impatiently waiting
For that fish with little red fins . . .

Ah today
By the lake
I lean back against the newly painted bench
How long shall I wait sitting here?
Again and once again
I ask myself . . .

Placement

To my left is a wax banana.
If I put down my pen
I can walk into the dusky stillness of night.

To my right is a clay bird.
I practice
My talent of drinking without talking.

At my feet sits my son,
Forever rearranging his battle lines.
May he be an unfilial son.

Behind me you stand,
Now bending over me, now resolutely walking
    away.
Yes, I do like only men with strong will.

Friends part, scattered in all directions.
There's no need to write;
Just stiffen your face and send the greetings.

The wicked draw near and hide.
All other shadows darting back and forth
Give me immense pleasure.

Sun and moon forever on the move,
Only I alone sit utterly still
Facing a pile of blank papers.

Xiao Kang
(1945 –   )

A native of Funing County in Jiangsu,
after graduating from the Literature De-
partment of Harbin's Helongjiang Uni-
versity, she did editorial work for the
literary journal *Northern Literature*. La-
ter she was a journalist with the
Guangming Daily in Beijing. Currently
she is editor of *Poetry Journal* in Beijing.
Her poems have appeared in literary
magazines and newspapers since 1978.
Xiao's poetic collections include a long
narrative poem, *The Bronze Sculpture*,
and two volumes of lyric poems, *The
Scattered Flower Leaves* and *Venus*.

Eyes

When you lower your head,
  Your long lashes
Screen the shadow;
When you glance around,
  The warmth in your gaze
Brings stirring discoveries;
When you gaze,
  Your sparkling eyes
Reveal a shy speech;
When you close your eyes
  The universe resounds
In a soothing lullaby.

You are the soul's window
Storing thunderstorms.
Having you, I can bury
All squabbles and nags;
Having you, I've tasted
Honeyed silence.

Ah, let me look straight at you,
Listening to your eternal refrain,
Let me walk close to you, walking
From your eyes to the bottom of your heart.

Sleep

My dear, please move away your arm
For I'm not used to, nor need
To fall asleep pillowing on it.
Don't linger in

Any silken entanglement,
Don't be drowned in a
Drunkenness that ensnares like a net, just
Save a little for the deep starry skies
Save a little for the rippling springwater
For sleep is a storehouse of energy
Don't let the springtime of youth
Wither in vain in the fire of passion.

My dear, please remove your arm,
Daytime din has ceased
Leaving only the night wind whistling
May your dream be a land on heroic shore
Forever blooming with fresh flowers and birds
    soaring
May my dream be a deep, deep sea
Where ships forever voyage to distant places
Then let us meet in our dreams
Ah sleep is life's germination
Let life's sweet wine be eternally
Brimming in the golden cup of new life.

My dear, please remove your arm
Let me say 'good night'
Drowsiness has descended
Oh, I long for sleep, for sleep.

The Wave and the Shoal

The small boat is grounded in the shallows
They've found the most isolated place
Everything disappears from the world
Only two souls singing,
Join the chorus of waves and shoals.

He silently ponders: that wave
How like a deeply loving girl
Charmed by the shoal she gently strokes his
    shoulders
And when she's stricken in his bosom of the
    shoal
How splendidly bloom the sea flowers . . .

She quietly muses: that shoal,
How like a lovesick young man
Loving the wave, he begs her to be his bride
Forever passionately in love,
Sharing one seabed . . .

Ah, lovesick shoal . . .
Ah, loving wave . . .
Her fine hair flowing in his arm's bay
He's drowned in her subtly heady fragrance.
Everything disappears in this world
Only the wave and the shoal pouring out their
    songs.

Fire and Ice

Fire are you
And ice I am
Having met you
How can it not melt
This long kept, unquenchable tenderness?

Fire are you
And ice I am
In the sunlight
I gaze upon

Your burning flame
Its shine and transparency
And you, are you savouring
The snowflake's gleaming love
Pulsing beneath the light?

Fire are you
And ice I am
Doubting not the spells love casts
Hiding not the crazed outpourings of love
In the stillness of night
Beneath the shivering stars
It will quietly shout aloud
Crystal —
Soul's crystal
Whether it is fire
Or ice
Who can resist passionately loving
— Such innocence
— Such luminescence?

Xiao Min
(1955 –   )

Born in Guangzhou Xiao Min worked
for the telegraph company in Guang-
zhou in 1968 and started to publish her
poetry and prose in 1973. Ten years la-
ter she was transferred to work for the
Guangdong branch of the Chinese Writ-
ers' Association. Her book of poems
Flowers Like Ivory was published in the
same year (1983). Her second book of
verse, *The Bottled Boat*, came out in
1986.

They, the Women

Even the street lamps are tired,
Feebly blinking their eyes to stay awake.
Over the clodded brick streets,
They walk to their night-shifts;
   They've just put their thumb-sucking toddlers
   In cots at the daycare center;
   Just unwillingly flung on their heavy uniforms
   After folding away their light skirts;
   Steamed ready the buns and dumplings
   For their families' meals tomorrow;
   Just taken leave of the old ones' sickbeds
   And counted the countless ration coupons for
     rice, oil . . .

Everyone is sound asleep.
But they walk on, rubbing their sleepy eyes,
Cursing the evening breeze that refuses to sing.
Even the breeze is asleep,
Only a few weary stars are left in the sky.
And on the streets trudged smooth by feet,
They walk to their night-shifts,
   They've just parted from the white swan
   Gliding with such grace in the play;
   Just solved a few equations bending
   Over desks;
   Just locked carefully away their sons' diplomas
   In the newly acquired dresser;
   Just blushed a response to that strange
   Annoying enquiry on the cool steps . . .

Everything is stilled, profoundly still.
But they merrily walk together,
Embarking on a journey between today and
   tomorrow.

And I am one of them,
The curly-haired girl who believes men can fly;
I am one of them,
The one mother who tells stories about mer-
     maids,
I am that one magical lantern
Forever elusive, forever aflame.
I'm the nightingale guarding the night passage,
Visible only to them.
     All my songs are sung for them,
     All my poems are written, entirely
     Written
     For them.

Flowers Like Ivory

Swinging a white shirt
You entered through the rays slanting in the
     window,
And drew a line down the middle of the desk we
     shared,
While I took offense and pouted.
In your notebook you sketched warships and
     knights on horseback
And nudged my elbow to copy my maths.
Wagging a finger you tried to shame me
For crying when I fell.
Then seeing no one looking,
You helped me up and told me
You knew of a flower like ivory
Which would heal my knees.

One day, the line between us disappeared,

And in my drawer I found a bunch of flowers
    like ivory.
The wind had carried you far, far away,
Because your father was in some kind of trouble
About which no one was too clear.

The creamy flowers withered;
I scattered the petals in the yard,
Hoping that they would sprout and grow;
Their new fragrant petals would hold
The ivory memories of my childhood.

We met again one day
At the place where you'd gathered the flowers,
Averting your eyes, you shuffled over
In a pair of old gym shoes.
You talked about the tiny village in the moun-
    tains,
Where you quarried stone, built walls and dug
    wild taro;
About the cracked terraced fields and parched
    ears of grain,
And the ploughs pulled by men till this day.
I mentioned the ivory flowers still in my drawer.
Silently you walked towards the setting sun,
Turning back after a dozen steps.
Softly you picked the creamy wind-blown petals
    from my hair;
And, when I stood amazed,
Quickly put them in a notebook.

Then I entered university
And wrote many poems which I considered
    beautiful,
Though I never dared write about you.
By chance, a friend mentioned having seen you
    in prison.

Was it because of that Qingming* night,
Or your comments on the man-drawn plough?
In the prison you secretly wrote poems;
I never knew you also wrote
About the stream under the ice,
The seeds in the warm earth
And longings for and memories of those ivory
  flowers.

I closed the door and wept.
Tearfully, I painted a bunch of ivory flowers and
  framed them.
At night, the flowers were intoxicatingly fragrant,
As you stood on the other side of the figured
  glass,
Wagging a finger to shame me
For crying when I hadn't fallen
And sighing for the losses of youth and faith
In the modern lines I composed.
You asked me if I remembered
Where the creamy flowers had grown
And the recollections and longings they aroused.

I searched and searched for you . . .
Backing the setting sun, I dropped my head,
Thinking of the suffering and significance of
  walking all night till dawn.
I gathered the seeds of the ivory flowers and scat-
  tered them everywhere
Hoping you'd do the same.
When your seeds and mine
Sprouted together in the warm earth,
Their resilient vines entangled

---

*At Qingming Festival, 5th April 1976, a day when the Chinese
commemorate their dead, people went to Tiananmen Square to
mourn the death of the late Premier Zhou. Many were arrested
on the orders of the 'gang of four'.

In the morning rays,
I would hear you whispering, 'Please blossom.
Let purity and fragrance disperse the mist
And spread far and wide!'

Would you not shame me again
When I put the new creamy petals in an envelope
And disclosed this ivory secret of mine? . . .

August 1982
Translated by Yu Fanqin

My Wall

I brush away at my
Milk-white wall.
My arms go up and down
Vigorously brushing,
My feet are planted on the wooden ladder
That teeters slightly under me.

I brush away the little fighting men
Pencilled on the wall;
I brush away the half sun formed
By a half moon and a few lines, unable to rise;
I brush away eighteen horizontal beams
That stand tall behind the door.
I brush away at my
Milk-white wall.

Wanting my wall to be gleaming clean again,
I must pay with strength I never had before.
To take the place of the milky whiteness
There will be greens, tender as young shoots,
Not gray,

Or dusky yellow.
I toil, I'm weary
But that soft green will ripen,
Doggedly grow and spread
Under my caring hands.

O my wall
Will be gleaming clean again!
Leaning against the door
Like powerful pillar,
I solemnly
Ponder . . .

Xu Hui
(1953 –   )

Born in Chendu, Sichuan, and daughter
of parents who are both teachers, Xu
grew up during the turbulent era of the
'cultural revolution'. Not quite sixteen
years of age, Xu was sent to work in the
countryside. After her return to the city
in 1974 she became a factory worker and
started to publish her poetry. Since
her graduation from the Chinese Depart-
ment of the Sichuan University, Xu has
worked for a literary monthly. Her book
of poems *A Bouquet of Poetic Blossoms*
won her a prize from the poetry journal
The Stars.

The Great River Severed: An Impression

Two long dikes stretch to the middle of the river
— Two partners met by chance,
Reaching out for strength and friendship . . .

Again and again the river dashed forward
But failed to dash their hopes.
At last hand in hand they hold on firmly;
A thunderous echo resounds between heaven
      and earth . . .

Out of this warm encounter burst forth the
      blazing sparks
The light ones, rising skyward, change to count-
      less stars;
The heavier ones, falling to the ground,
Change to two banks of street lamps.

The Ancient Passageway

Was it to find lost sheep in a dream
Or to seek that crimson cloud
Beyond the ravine
Where my indomitable forefathers
Chiseled out this passage with their bloody
      hands —
Half way up the steep cliff of a thousand feet
A slender rope afloat in mid-air?
Ah, within the Kui Gate the soil is rich.
Wild roses blooming white on the boughs
Tug at your sleeves,
The hill stream whispers:

O stop, please stop,
Don't go forward . . .

Seeds scattered by nature
Take root on every piece of soil,
But you have let a deep blue hope
Make its steep climb along this perilous passage,
— to the strange world
Ah, these vague longings are
Not merely for surviving.

Yang Liuhong
(1965 –   )

Born in Beijing but a native of Wuxi, Jiangsu, Yang spent her childhood years during the decade of political turmoil of the 'cultural revolution' in various cadre schools in the villages where her parents were sent. In 1986 she graduated from the Population Department of the Chinese People's University. Currently she is on the staff of the Social Institute of that university. Her poems have appeared in a number of literary magazines since 1981; they are also collected in *White Sand Island*.

The White Sand Island

That's the White Sand Island! Have you been
    there?
See how they glimmer, those white sands:
Cradle of the pearly shells
Pleasure garden of the stars
Dreamland of corals

The sun's reveries are red, the moon's are white
The sun mysteriously blazes its beauty
The moon truthfully bares her loveliness
The moon's mirror is the island whose mirror is
    the sun

Since you are a minstrel I urge you to journey
    there
It isn't too far — just beyond the sea, by the sky's
    edge
I've just come from there, my feet are still sandy
The 'I' of today isn't the 'I' of yesterday
I've lost and found many things that I've
    sought in vain:
A gull's wings
A seastar's rudder
A shellfish's sail
A sea soul tied with streamers

I've learned to laugh, forgetting how to cry
A child can not tell crying from laughing
But I'm not a child, I know the difference
Now I'm all grown up
Unlike yesterday
Screaming for Mother when hit by a head wind
I know the briny taste of seawind
I know too much honey will taste bitter . . .

Once there was a mermaid moonbathing
In moonlight glinting like white sands
That now gently support me
I'm no Sleeping Beauty with age-old hair as long
   as sea breeze
But do you recognize me?
I can still shout and dash about
Will you laugh with me when I'm tickled?

This is the White Sand Island, this is me
Tied to fluttering streamers, my soul
And the sea soul exist together

To a Butterfly Specimen

No longer able to fly
You yet offer men the dream of flight;
No longer able to dream
You yet offer men the memories of summer;
No longer able to remember
You yet immortalize all memories.
Ages later when men
See you again
They will surely realize
Your memories, your dreams . . .

Yi Lei

(1951 –   )

A native of Tianjin, Yi was sent to work in the agricultural farms upon her graduation from middle school in 1969. Two years later she was a reporter for the liberation army as well as a staff member of the newspaper *The Railway Corps*. Yi has attended classes in creative writing in Hebei, at the Lu Xun Academy, and at Beijing University. Since her first appearance on the literary scene in 1974, she has published two books of poems, *The Flames of Love* and *Love's Formula*.

Meeting the Seagull Again

Out of a haze of fog a white crack splits open,
Ah gull, you've fallen from the sky!
A whitecap with eyes has now joined the sea,
Freely it selects its own direction.

O seagull, my angel of freedom!
You go when you want to go,
You come when you want to come.
Have you visited the sky over Victoria Bay?
Have you followed the white waves of motor
     boats on the East Sea?
Have you tasted the grains in the valleys of the
     Yellow Sea?
Which world-famous rivers have you cruised?
All these are your secrets,
There's no need for me to know, for you to
     answer.

Once I imagined that you were a comet's tail
My heart, borne on your bright long wing,
Skimmed across the stars' darkening plain and
I felt as if I'd touched the frightful brink of the
     universe.
Seagull, you are fated to disappear,
For what am I fated to wait?
I lie down, lying, I lie transformed into a golden
     shore,
The moving autumn waves have hardened into
     rocks,
But I, I cannot curse you
Because though we may be fated for life,
There's no contract to bind us.

My eyes greedily pursue you through fogs and
     clouds.

O have we known each other before?
Have we met before?
No, it is a miracle that we meet today.
In life's fleeting voyage, how can one hope to
    meet twice?!
Now we meet, now we part. This is the order of
    the universe.
O seagull, like wind, like fog, no need for us to
    say goodbye.
Parting, I thank you for the glorious moment you
    gave me.

Between Strangers

Stranger, who can measure the distance be-
    tween us?
As great as the distance between Europe and the
    Pacific Ocean?
Perhaps it is but an infinitely thin space,
So thin that a match
Can illuminate our two strange worlds,
Perhaps face to face for an instant
One can then cross over this nonexistent door-
    way,
Perhaps when sensitive fingers come to meet
Two hearts will pluck a hushed chord of har-
    mony.
Perhaps a continuous stream of footprints upon
    footprints
May erase a tough line of defense at a lonely
    crossing,
Perhaps a humble courteous yielding
May enable both sides to attain to all rights,

Ah stranger perhaps when nothing happens
We may yet pass through many good turns
Each goes on his chosen path
Till death without exchanging a word with each
    other.
Surely, the encounter of two brilliant ideas is
    possible!
But nothing has happened.
And because we're strangers we cannot regret for
    not having met,
Yet this kind of regret permeates all our lives.

Yi Lin
(1948 –   )

Born in the Xiaoshan County of Zhe-
jiang, Yi Lin grew up by the beautiful
West Lake of Hangzhou and graduated
from the Chinese Department of Hang-
zhou University. Upon graduation she
served as editor of the literary monthly
The Eastern Sea until she was transferred
to work for the Zhejiang branch of the
Chinese Writers' Association in 1987, the
year she also entered the Lu Xun Acade-
my for further studies. Since she began
to publish her work in 1978, Yi has
completed several volumes of verse in-
cluding *My March Eighth*, *White Butter-
fly* and *Wild Duck*.

My Heart

My heart is lucid and spotless
Like a transparent glass.
When you gently brush it with deep sentiments,
It will clearly image forth your soul
But don't ever step on it with heartless shoes
Because it is very fragile
As fragile as a thin piece of glass.

Dandelion

A gentle breath
Asks the breeze to carry you high.
Once ripened, it is time to leave,
Then why this insistent delay?

I was once envious of the wind,
I was once envious of the bright clouds,
The heart holds too many teardrops,
Can anyone understand my feeling?

Fly away, O, fly away!
Since you've ceased lingering.
The little white bird
Belongs to the sky's eternal blue.

Yu Xiaoping
(1955 –   )

Born in Nanjing, Yu worked as an art
designer for the Nanjing Chinese Opera
Group upon her graduation from middle
school in 1971. Ten years later she en-
tered the Nanjing Creative Writing Insti-
tute and began to publish her poems and
songs. Since 1984 Yu has been working
for the Jiangsu branch of the Chinese
Writers' Association.

On an Autumn Day I Stroll
Along a Reedbank

On an autumn day I stroll along a reedbank.

The river, a silvery brocade, flows slowly on
   Overflowing perhaps with the sail's heavy
      cargo of stories,
Or is it scrutinizing me — a curly-haired girl
   dressed in lavender,
   Carrying a portfolio of paintings on her back?

What secrets could the wind
   Be whispering to those giddy girls, the reeds.
They burst into such laughter their slender waists
   bend all askew.
   Ah their genial intimacy both charms and
      moves me.

Then there's an old fisherman chanting an
   ancient ditty,
   His net has bobbed joy and defeats of his old
      age.
I remember my grandfather humming the same
   tune
   Perhaps this is where they used to wade and
      play as children

The freshly harvested field baring its bosom
Like my childhood playmate — a young mother
   after delivery
   Finally relaxed after a long painful battle,
Submerged in a dreamland of blissful mother-
   hood

An unending dike extends endlessly my reverie
   That gallops unbridled across the vast cerulean
     void
The drifting dust flares up refrains of memories.
   Overhead, a proud sun is mellowing at high
     noon.

On an autumn day I stroll along the reedbank

Zhai Yongming
(1955 –   )

A native of Chendu, Sichuan Province, Zhai graduated from the Chendu Electric Communication Engineering Institute and now she works at Chendu Literary Institute. Zhai has published works since 1981.

Monologues

I, a crazy idea, filled with the abyss's subtle power
By chance was given birth by you. Earth and
    heaven
Then mingled into one. You called me woman.
You strengthened my body.

I am a white feather, soft as water
You hold me in your hand and I hold the
    world in mine.
Clothed in this earthly flesh, how dazzling I am
In the sunlight. You find this incredible.

I am a most tender, understanding woman.
I see through everything, accepting everything.
I yearn for winter, an immense dark night.
With the heart as the boundary I desire to hold
    your hand
But before you my poise is a tragic defeat.

When you walk away, my pain
Heaves out my heart.
To slay you with love, whose denial is this?
The sun rises for the whole world! For you
I fill your entire body, from head to toe,
With the most belligerent tenderness.
I have my formula.

A clamor of cries for help. Can a soul stretch out
    its arms?
With the oceans a bloodstream I would be raised
Beneath the feet of the setting sun. Does some-
    one remember me?
What I remember, absolutely, is not merely one
    lifetime.

Zhang Ye
(1948-)

A native of Fenghua of Zhejiang Province, Zhang was born in Shanghai. Because of illness Zhang had to stay at home after her graduation from high school in 1966. Since her graduation from the Chinese Department of the Shanghai University in the early 1980s, she has been teaching at the same university. Although she started writing in 1965, Zhang did not start publishing her poems until 1982. Her first book of poems, *A Poet's Love*, appeared in 1986.

My Car Passes Sweet Love Street

It's early spring
On parasol branches leaped tender hope,
The car raced on the newly tarred street.
A voice came chasing after the car
Calling my name.

The car passed by Sweet Love Street, not stopping
Holding on tight to the shaking handle, not
    uttering a sound
As if unsure of my coming. Why did I get
All dressed up so elegantly?
Why over my shirt did I stealthily
Pin a spring orchid with such clear scent?
Why the quivers in my breast, the burning
    cheeks?

But they all know,
The parasol tree smiling by the roadside,
And the birds I used to know in the old days.

My car has passed by Sweet Love Street,
Making no stop, I uttered not a single sound
But the sky in my heart is raining, raining.

Divorce

Sadly she smiles
Taking away their five-year-old child.
Waves ripple in his eyes,
A lone boat floats in the water.

The child's heading far and farther with mother.
Holding his father's shadow,
The delicate little hands
Have crushed the sweet chocolate.

A dim instant
Has kindled unfading memories.

Zheng Ling
(1931 –   )

Born in the Jiangjin County of Sichuan, Zheng joined the staff of the Creative Writing Division of the Workers' Cultural Troupe in Changsha in Hunan in 1950. Two years later she became a literature editor of the Hunan People's Publishing House. She is now on the staff of the Federation of Literary and Art Circles of Zhuzhou. Zheng began writing poetry in the 1950s and she has since published two books of poems: *Selected Poems of Zheng Ling* and *Songs of Little Mermaid*. Her poems have been admired for their power and profundity.

Conversing with the Sea

Gazing at the great expanse of swirling mists and
    waves,
I fall on my knees, awed by the sea's grandeur.
I ask: O sea
Of all your riches, what do you cherish the most?
The sea replies:
Some say my pearls
Which are in truth a mermaid's tears,
Some say my color
Which is in truth the beauty of the blue skies.
What I cherish most
Is a drop of water that slips into my bosom
From a crack in the rock

Love of Lake Dongting

Where did I come from?
Why once we've met can I not bear to leave you?
Gazing at your endless stretch of billowing field
I suddenly forget my own puny shape.
At first I was only a small boat with no sail or
    mast,
Unwilling to anchor in a dirty harbor
Now I toss myself on to your windswept waves
And find communion in your immeasurable
    depths
As if since the dawn of creation
We've existed side by side.

Your misty waves are brimless, borderless,
There's no beginning, no ending.
At first, I came searching to quench my thirst
But instead I lose myself in your boundlessness.
I — A fretful ghost of crazed love
A slave of jealousy,
For years unreconciled with fate
But now before your vast expanse of deep greens
I feel no honor, shame, gratitude or grievance
Worthy to be mentioned.

I only wish to be a meteor in the depth of night
Burning with all my heart
Piercing through the sky's darkness
To land in your heart's waves
Let your flowing water
Mirror my last wink of light
Then fading into your bosom
Find my peace.

Zheng Min
(1920 –   )

A native of Minhou County, Fujian,
Zheng graduated from the Philosophy
Department of the Southwest Joint Uni-
versity in wartime Kunming in 1943.
That same year she went abroad to stu-
dy at Brown University in the United
States. In 1952 she received her M.A.
degree. Since her return to China in
1955, Zheng has been actively pursuing
both a writing and academic career of
research and teaching. At present she is
a professor of English at the Teachers'
College in Beijing. She has published
two books of poems, *Collected Poems:
1942-1947* and *Seeking,* and one volume
of critical essays, *A Study of British and
American Poetry and Plays.* Her poems
have also been collected in *Nine Leaves*
and *Eight Leaves.*

Silkworms

A whole life is concentrated in these magical
    black dots
Which turn overnight into a mass of short
    threads,
Swimming in a green sea of tender leaves
And growing into tender round flesh
With slender bodies and tiny crimson mouths.

In an unceasing rustle
Making towards the precious transparence,
You rear up, intoxicated
By thoughts and fancies of tomorrow,
Planning the construction
Of tomorrow's white palace.

To construct a future with your lives,
For a renascence after death,
With long silver fibers
You bind your flesh over and over,
It is a stage in life,
Awaiting advance in retreat.

At all events,
Your transparent dwellings
Are neither dormitories
Nor much less tombs,
Life pulsates inside,
In the water's turbulence you exchange death
For the continuity of silver threads in time and
    space.

Translated by Bonnie S. McDougall

Hope and Dashed Hope

Hope, hope, where can I find hope?
Between the collapse of two waves,
Between two rippled peaks,
And in the valley of waves, there hides hope.

If hope's peak never sinks into valleys,
Sea shall lose its existence, for a waveless sea is
A breathless bosom that breathes nothing but
    death,
No matter how heroic, how grand it appears.

History falls from crest to trough,
And from trough rises to crest again.
Hope is our helmsman
When we sink into the rippled valley,

Wall of waves seeks to bury our small craft,
And dashed hopes seek to toss us into the abyss.
We've climbed atop the billowing peak.
Let red sun fill the cabin, sea breeze fill the sail.

A Cloud of Hair Gleaming in Spring

(Wu Guxiang's 'Portrait of a Lady', Qing Dynasty)

This painter gave you a cloud of hair
Set high upon your head;
A tight silk gown, sleeves broadly loose
But like a water scallion
Yellowish green, and fragile
Your eyes, softly drawn, capture
A soul suffocating inside.

You only stare at the jade hairpin in your hand.
Such pitiful life behind the lovely pose
Even the sighs are forgotten.
The naked cries and desires of youth
Have long been smothered in silk and brocade.
   Sunlight
Though radiant in spring
Cannot pierce this elegant coldness
That people used to wrap your flesh with;
Pale ribbons strangling your veins.
Oh you cold, cold woman
If only you could rip apart this silk
And leap back into the sea of life
To recover the lost pulse.
To love, to hate in the flesh is far far better
Than this life's token — a jade hairpin.

Index of First Lines